INSIDE BATTLESHIPS

Thanks to the creative team:
Senior Editor: Alice Peebles
Fact Checking: Tom Jackson
Illustrations: Mat Edwards and Victor Mclindon
Picture Research: Nic Dean
Design: www.collaborate.agency

Original edition copyright 2017 by Hungry Tomato Ltd.
Copyright © 2018 by Lerner Publishing Group, Inc.

Hungry Tomato® is a trademark of Lerner Publishing Group

All rights reserved. International copyright secured. No part of this book may be reproduced, stored in a retrieval system, or transmitted in any form or by any means—electronic, mechanical, photocopying, recording, or otherwise—without the prior written permission of Lerner Publishing Group, Inc., except for the inclusion of brief quotations in an acknowledged review.

Hungry Tomato®
A division of Lerner Publishing Group, Inc.
241 First Avenue North
Minneapolis, MN 55401 USA

For reading levels and more information, look up this title at www.lernerbooks.com.

Main body text set in Avenir Next Condensed Medium 11/15.
Typeface provided by Linotype AG.

Library of Congress Cataloging-in-Publication Data

Names: Oxlade, Chris, author.
Title: Inside battleships / Chris Oxlade.
Description: Minneapolis : Hungry Tomato, [2017] | Series: Inside military machines | Includes index. | Audience: Grades 4-6. | Audience: Ages 8-12.
Identifiers: LCCN 2017014445 (print) | LCCN 2017012916 (ebook) | ISBN 9781512450026 (eb pdf) | ISBN 9781512432251 (lb : alk. paper)
Subjects: LCSH: Battleships–Juvenile literature. | Warships–Juvenile literature.
Classification: LCC V815 (print) | LCC V815 .O93 2017 (ebook) | DDC 623.825–dc23

LC record available at https://lccn.loc.gov/2017014445

Manufactured in the United States of America
1-41780-23541-4/3/2017

INSIDE BATTLESHIPS

An *Iowa*-class World War II battleship fires her guns in action.

by Chris Oxlade

Minneapolis

USS *Texas*, a huge battleship that fought in both world wars

Contents

Battle Machines: Battleships	6
The First Warships	8
Ancient Sea Battles	10
Medieval Warships	12
Ships of the Line	14
Ironclads	16
Battleships	18
The Rise of Carriers	20
Modern Warships	22
Modern Aircraft Carriers	24
Inside a Warship	26
Timeline	28
Fact File	29
Glossary	30
Index	32

BATTLE MACHINES: BATTLESHIPS

Warships are the weapons of a navy, which is a country's military force at sea. These battle machines protect their own ships and attack enemy ships, aircraft, and forces ashore. Since their invention, there have been dozens of different types of warship. These days, the main types are **frigates**, destroyers, cruisers, and aircraft carriers—the largest of all modern battleships.

USS *Nimitz* aircraft carrier

Battle of Trafalgar, 1805

Old and New

The two pictures show how warships have changed over time. Above is British Vice Admiral Nelson's ship **HMS** *Victory* with other ships of the line at the Battle of Trafalgar. These were wooden sailing ships armed with dozens of cannons. On the left is the steel supercarrier **USS** *Nimitz*. Its weapons are its devastating strike aircraft, so this enormous ship presents a whole new world of battleship technology.

THE FIRST WARSHIPS

Nobody knows who invented the first boat, but it was invented more than ten thousand years ago. Early boats were simple craft made of logs or bundles of reeds, but slowly boat builders learned to build bigger boats. They also invented new technologies such as sails and oars. As long as four thousand years ago, specialized warships were going into battle.

Egyptian Warships

There are pictures of sailing boats on the Nile River in Egypt, painted about 5,500 years ago, with **hulls** made from reed bundles. Similar boats, armed with soldiers, could have been the first battleships. The Egyptians soon developed strong, seaworthy **merchant ships** made of wood. Warships called **galleys** were based on these merchant ships, but galleys were longer, narrower, and faster. They carried archers and spearmen for attacking enemy craft.

Triremes

The most powerful warship of Ancient Greece was the trireme, a galley powered by three banks of oars on each side. These big ships had a strong **keel** along the length of the boat, with frames to support planking for the hull. The trireme became the main Greek fighting ship. Later ships had catapults on board for firing huge darts and stones at the enemy.

Uniremes and Biremes

The earliest warships built by the Ancient Greeks were galleys called uniremes. The main weapon was a ram sticking out from the **bow**. The ram was used to smash enemy ships before soldiers boarded to fight the enemy's crew. Around 750 BCE, the Greeks developed the bireme, with two banks of oars for better speed.

Trireme Rowers

A typical trireme had three rows of twenty-five or more oars on each side, making at least one hundred fifty in total. The oarsmen sat on different levels inside the hull, sliding backward and forward on leather cushions as they rowed. The crews had to be well-trained to row fast and move their ships accurately in battle. Some navies experimented with massive galleys with a thousand or more rowers!

Greek Trireme

Length: 125 feet (38 meters)

Width: 20 feet (6 m)

Crew: 200

Oars: 170

Top speed: 8 miles (13 kilometers) per hour

ANCIENT SEA BATTLES

The great powers of the ancient world, including the Greeks, Romans, and Persians, all built large fleets of fighting galleys. When the navies met in battle, hundreds of opposing biremes and triremes would try to ram and sink each other, and there would be fierce hand-to-hand fighting on deck. Among the greatest battles was the Battle of Salamis, in 480 BCE.

The Battle of Salamis

Salamis was a great sea battle between the Greek and Persian navies during the Greco-Persian Wars. The battle took place off the Greek coast, in the channel between the island of Salamis and the port of Piraeus. The Greeks, who had about three hundred seventy galleys, lured the bigger Persian force (about eight hundred galleys) into the narrow strait and then attacked, sinking three hundred Persian ships while losing just forty of their own.

Salamis Key Facts

When:	480 BCE
Where:	Greece
Number of ships:	800 Persian / 370 Greek
Losses:	300 Persian ships / 40 Greek ships
Winner:	Greece

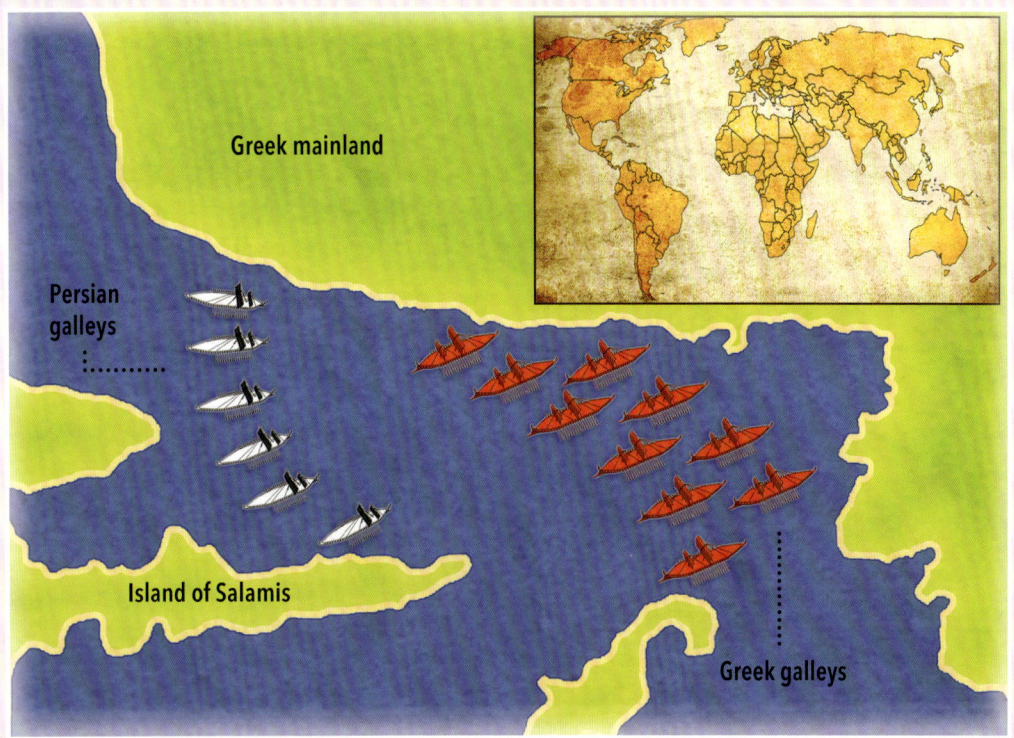

Battle Tactics

The Greeks won the Battle of Salamis because the Persian ships could not maneuver in the narrow waters where the Greeks chose to attack them. Rowing at top speed, the Greeks rammed into the Persian ships, putting holes in them and stopping them from escaping. Greek soldiers swarmed onto the rammed ships and captured or sank them.

Greek Fire

A new weapon was introduced in battles between galleys more than one thousand years after Salamis. It was invented in the seventh century CE and was called Greek fire. The main ingredient was oil or tar. It was heated, ignited, and squirted through a nozzle at enemy ships, setting them ablaze and causing panic.

MEDIEVAL WARSHIPS

Warships changed very little between ancient times and medieval times about one thousand years later. The ships continued to have a single square sail and lots of oars. But in the twelfth and thirteenth centuries, new ship technologies were invented such as the **stern rudder**, deep keel, triangular sail, and full rigging. These made ships more maneuverable and able to sail against the wind. Guns were also invented, so by the fifteenth century there were large, strong warships with three masts, armed with rows of deadly cannons.

mixture of square and triangular sails

sterncastle

stern rudder

The Armada

The Spanish Armada was a large fleet sent to invade England in 1588. It included forty warships and nineteen thousand soldiers. While the Armada was at anchor, the English sent in ships set on fire, creating chaos. They then attacked with guns that had better range than those of the Spanish and defeated the Armada. It was one of first sea battles to feature cannons.

Ship's Cannon

The cannon was made possible by the invention of gunpowder. At first warships had cannons mounted only near the bow. Gradually, cannons got larger, and ships got more of them. The cannons were arranged along the sides of a ship, pointing out through gun ports. They fired iron cannonballs as heavy as 59.5 pounds (27 kilograms), which smashed and splintered the hulls and masts of enemy ships.

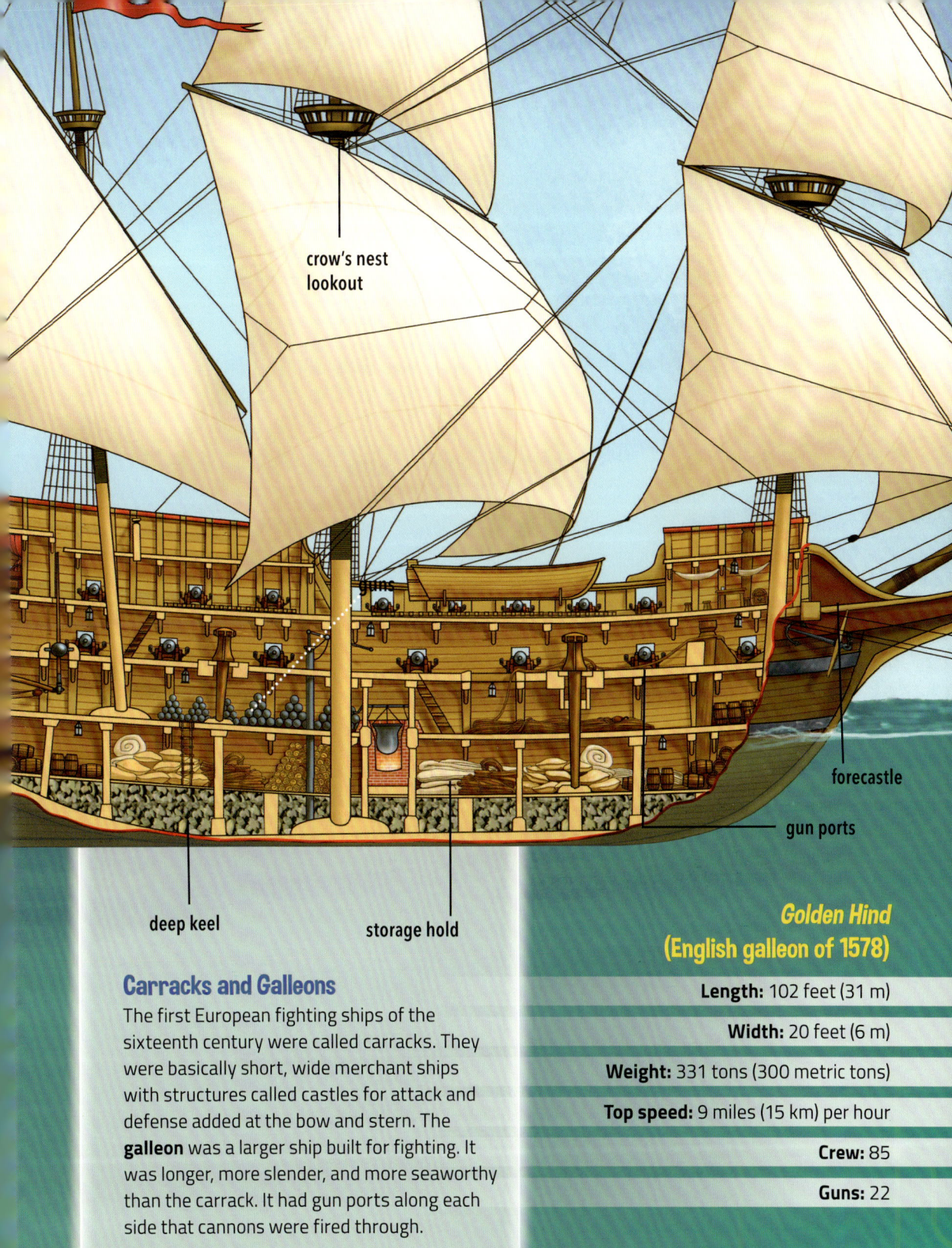

crow's nest lookout

forecastle

gun ports

deep keel

storage hold

Carracks and Galleons

The first European fighting ships of the sixteenth century were called carracks. They were basically short, wide merchant ships with structures called castles for attack and defense added at the bow and stern. The **galleon** was a larger ship built for fighting. It was longer, more slender, and more seaworthy than the carrack. It had gun ports along each side that cannons were fired through.

Golden Hind (English galleon of 1578)

Length: 102 feet (31 m)

Width: 20 feet (6 m)

Weight: 331 tons (300 metric tons)

Top speed: 9 miles (15 km) per hour

Crew: 85

Guns: 22

SHIPS OF THE LINE

The galleons of the sixteenth century were used for exploration and trading as well as for fighting. But by the seventeenth century, warships were specialized ships, built just for fighting. They had two or three gun decks and dozens of guns. These ships were known as great ships and later ships of the line because they fought in line formation, one behind the other.

HMS *Victory*

This is one of the gun decks of HMS *Victory*, a British ship that fought at Trafalgar. *Victory* was a first-rate ship of the line, with 104 guns. The guns rolled back on their carriages when they fired. During a battle, this deck would have been a terrifying place, filled with smoke, noise, and shouting as crews reloaded and fired their guns as quickly as possible.

The Battle of Trafalgar

By the start of the nineteenth century, sailing warships were powerful fighting machines, capable of terrible destruction. Major battles were fought between powerful ships of the line. At the Battle of Trafalgar in 1805, a fleet of twenty-seven British ships defeated thirty-three French and Spanish ships.

HMS *Prince*

Length: 131 feet (40 m)

Width: 45 feet (13.7 m)

Guns: 100

Crew: 780

HMS *Prince*

Built in 1670, *Prince* was one of the great ships of the English king, Charles II. The ship carried one hundred guns on three gun decks, with the biggest firing 42-pound (19 kg) cannonballs. *Prince* was not only deadly but also beautiful. It was covered in carvings and gold paint.

officer's quarters · crew quarters · masts down to the keel · rudder · gun deck · frame made of oak timbers

IRONCLADS

In the nineteenth century, the world of warships changed completely. Steam engines replaced sails as the main way to move ships, and big guns firing shells replaced cannons firing iron balls. Iron became available to shipbuilders, and soon wooden ships were covered in plates of thick iron armor. These were the **ironclads**. The American Civil War (1861–1865) saw some of the first battles between these new warships.

Ironclad Riverboat

This riverboat was built in 1856 to work as a ferry and river steamer on the Mississippi River in the United States. The US Army bought the boat in 1861, covered it in iron armor, added six guns, and renamed it USS *Essex*. The ship was in several fights with **Confederate** ships. It was damaged several times but never sank.

The Battle of Hampton Roads

One of the first ironclad battles was between USS *Monitor* and **CSS** *Virginia*. This battle took place near Hampton, Virginia, and became known as the Battle of Hampton Roads. *Monitor* and *Virginia* fired at each other, *Monitor* using its armored rotating turret gun. Both ships were damaged, but not badly, so the battle ended without a winner.

Confederate Ironclad

CSS *Virginia* was a Confederate ship in the American Civil War. It was built from the remains of a badly damaged wooden steam-powered frigate. Iron armor plates were added above the deck, there was a ram at the front, and guns were placed all around. The *Virginia* was one of the first warships to have a propeller rather than paddle wheels, which were used on previous steam-powered ships.

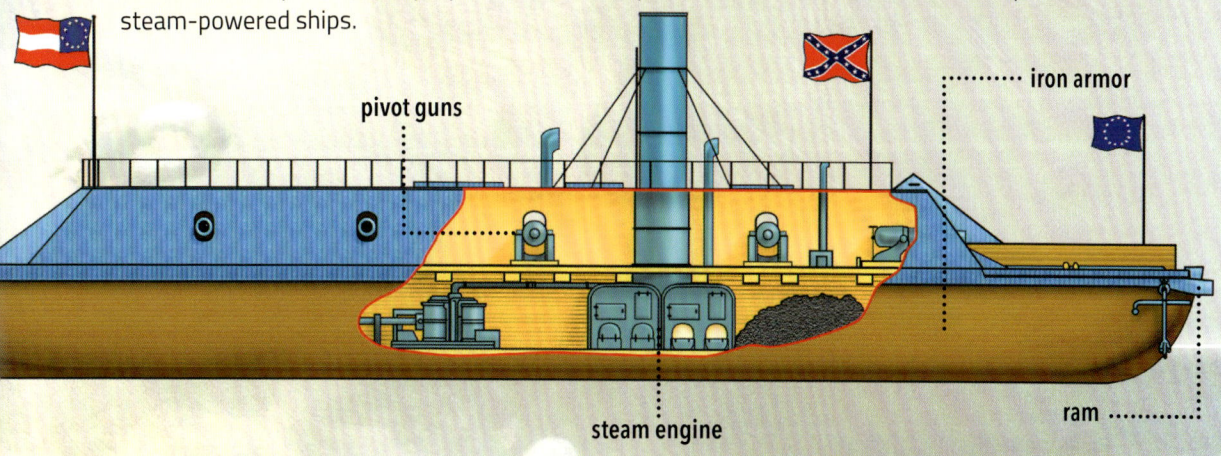

Breeches and Shells

Ironclads had a new type of gun. Unlike the cannons on ships of the line, the new guns were breech-loaders. They were loaded from the back instead of the front, which was much quicker and easier. They also fired exploding shells instead of solid balls. The shells were more accurate and flew farther than cannonballs.

CSS *Virginia*

Length: 276 feet (84 m)

Width: 52.5 feet (16 m)

Weight: 4,480 tons (4,064 metric tons)

Guns: 10

Crew: 320

BATTLESHIPS

By the beginning of the twentieth century, warships were not just clad with metal—they were made completely from metal. The biggest warships were covered with thick, hardened steel armor for protection against shells and **torpedoes**. They were armed with big guns that could hit targets more than 6 miles (10 km) away. These powerful ships were the first battleships.

USS *New Jersey*

This US Navy ship was the American version of the battleship and was similar to many battleships that served in World War I. It was armed with four 305 mm guns and eight 203 mm guns, and operated by 812 officers and men. The sides of the hull were painted in camouflage patterns to make the ship harder for submarines to spot against the waves.

HMS *Dreadnought*

One of the very first battleships was HMS *Dreadnought*. It was such a groundbreaking ship that battleships built after it were also known as dreadnoughts. HMS *Dreadnought* was launched in 1906. Along with its armor and big guns, it had a new type of engine—the **steam turbine**—to power its four propellers. These created much less vibration than normal steam engines and allowed a better top speed.

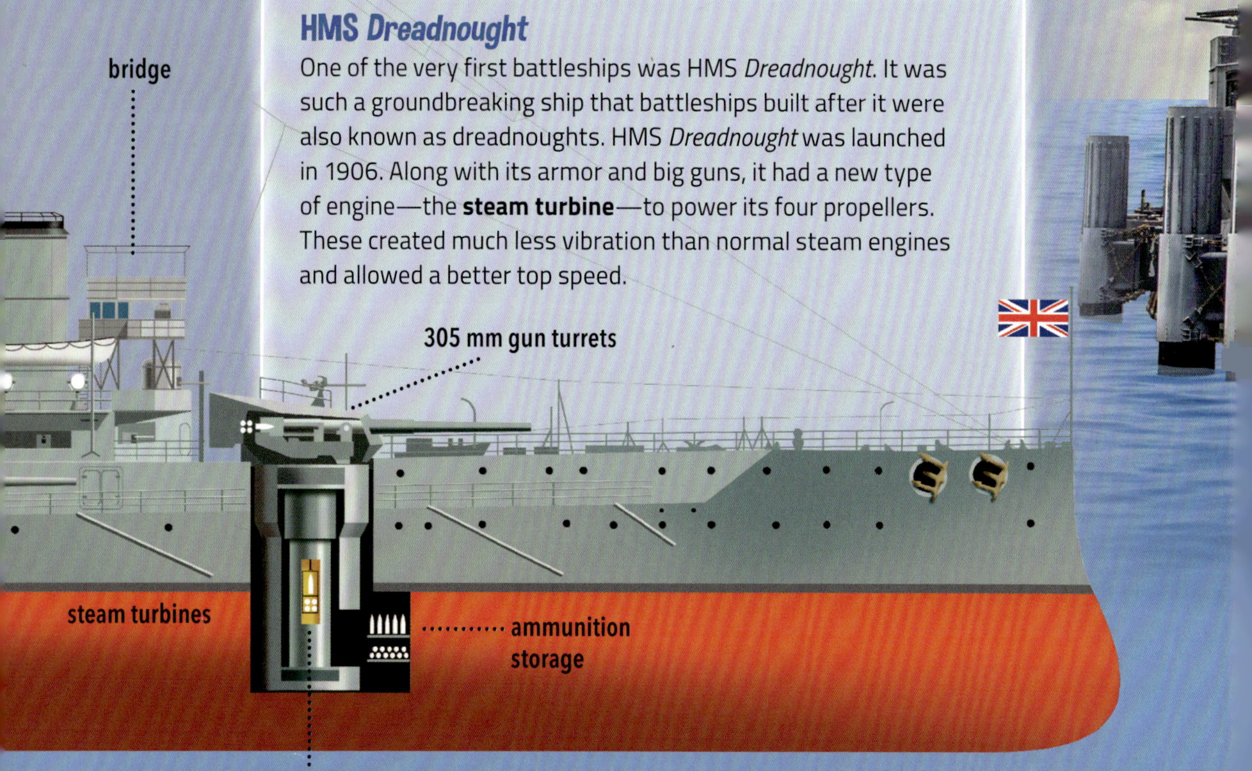

bridge

305 mm gun turrets

steam turbines

ammunition storage

ammunition elevator

HMS *Dreadnought*

Length: 348 feet (160 m)
Weight: 19,842 tons (18,000 metric tons)
Weapons: ten 305 mm guns
Crew: 800
Top speed: 24 miles (39 km) per hour

Two-War Ship

USS *Texas* entered service at the beginning of World War I (1914–1918). It was one of the most powerful battleships in the world. Its guns were very accurate, even when the ship was moving with the motion of the waves. It also fought in World War II (1939–1945), when it was fitted with antiaircraft guns, radar, and extra layers of hull armor to protect against torpedoes.

Torpedoes

Torpedoes, developed by English engineer Robert Whitehead in the 1860s, became powerful weapons. They were fired from the decks of warships, aimed to intercept an enemy ship. A spinning device inside the torpedoes kept them going in a straight line. By World War II, their range was about 4 miles (6 km), and their speed was about 50 miles (80 km) per hour.

THE RISE OF CARRIERS

The first experimental aircraft carriers were built around the end of World War I. They were made by adding flat decks on top of other warships or merchant ships. By the start of World War II, carriers were powerful weapons. They were important for forces fighting thousands of miles from home where there were no runways on land for aircraft to use. Their aircraft attacked enemy ships and targets on shore.

Carriers in the Pacific

American aircraft carriers operated in the Pacific Ocean during World War II, fighting Japanese forces. The USS *Essex* and its sister carriers weighed 30,313.5 tons (27,500 metric tons) and carried 100 aircraft. Later in the war even larger ships joined them. Planes from US carriers sank the Japanese battleships *Yamato* and *Musashi*, the two largest battleships ever built.

Battleship Barrage

Battleships such as the USS *Idaho* worked alongside aircraft carriers. In the Pacific battleships fought against Japanese battleships, protecting fleets of smaller ships. They also supported troops invading Pacific islands by attacking enemy defenses with their guns from far out at sea.

Runways at Sea

The top deck of a carrier is a runway used for takeoff and landing. The ship's bridge (control room) and the runway control tower is in the superstructure to the side of the deck. On World War II carriers, aircraft took off under their own power or were launched by a steam catapult. Landing was tricky, especially in rough weather, and required great skill from the pilots.

Hangars

Aircraft were stored on deck or in hangars under the flight deck, where they could be serviced and repaired. An elevator carried the planes between the deck and the hangar. Some ships had armored decks, and others had simple wooden decks that were easier to repair. Carrier aircraft had folding wings to save space on deck and in the hangar.

MODERN WARSHIPS

Modern navies operate a range of different warship types, each with its own role. There are small, fast attack craft, **mine** hunters, frigates, destroyers, and cruisers, which attack other ships and submarines and defend against aircraft and **missiles**. There are also giant aircraft carriers and assault ships for landing troops on beaches. The main weapons are missiles.

Stealth Ships

Many modern warships feature stealth technology, designed to make the ships difficult to detect. Like all stealth warships, this Swedish *Visby*-class corvette has flat surfaces on its hull and superstructure. This makes it hard for enemy radar systems to spot. It also has hidden exhaust outlets for its gas turbines, so that heat-seeking missiles can't find it. It carries remote-control **submersibles**, which search underwater for explosive mines.

Missile Defenses

The greatest threat to a modern warship is the antiship missile, fired from another ship or aircraft. Warships no longer have armor as battleships did. Instead they have antimissile and antiaircraft defenses that shoot down approaching airborne threats. These defenses include a close in weapons system (CIWS), which uses radar to track incoming missiles and aircraft, and a cannon that fires thousands of rounds per minute at the target to bring it down.

On the Bridge

A ship's crew controls the ships from the bridge, normally high up near the front of the ship. All the controls are electronic, and the ship is steered with small joysticks instead of steering wheels. This is the bridge of USS *Zumwalt*, a US Navy destroyer armed with **guided missiles**. Information from radars, cameras, and other equipment is displayed on monitors.

MODERN AIRCRAFT CARRIERS

Aircraft carriers are the biggest ships in modern naval fleets. They are incredibly powerful warships not because of onboard weapons but because of the aircraft they carry to attack targets in the air, at sea, and on land. These giant ships are moving air bases that can take the fight to any part of the world as part of a battle group.

Strike aircraft are stored on deck or in the hangar under the deck. Helicopters and reconnaissance planes are also carried.

The main flight deck has takeoff and landing areas.

antiaircraft and antimissile missiles

Deck Operations

Flight-deck crews organize aircraft for catapult takeoffs, landings, refueling, re-arming, servicing, and repairs. They move aircraft between the flight deck and hangar with four huge electrically powered elevators. Every crew member has a specific job to do and wears color-coded clothing to show what that job is.

Nimitz-class Carrier

The biggest aircraft carriers in the world belong to the US Navy. They are the *Nimitz*-class supercarriers such as the USS *John C. Stennis*, seen here operating in the Pacific Ocean. This carrier is powered by two nuclear reactors, which means it hardly ever has to refuel.

Nimitz-class Carrier

Length: 1092.5 feet (333 m)

Width: 253 feet (77 m)

Weight: 115,743 tons (105,000 metric tons)

Top speed: 35 miles (56 km) per hour

Propulsion: two nuclear reactors

Aircraft: 90 fixed wing aircraft and helicopters

Crew: 5,000

Range: almost unlimited

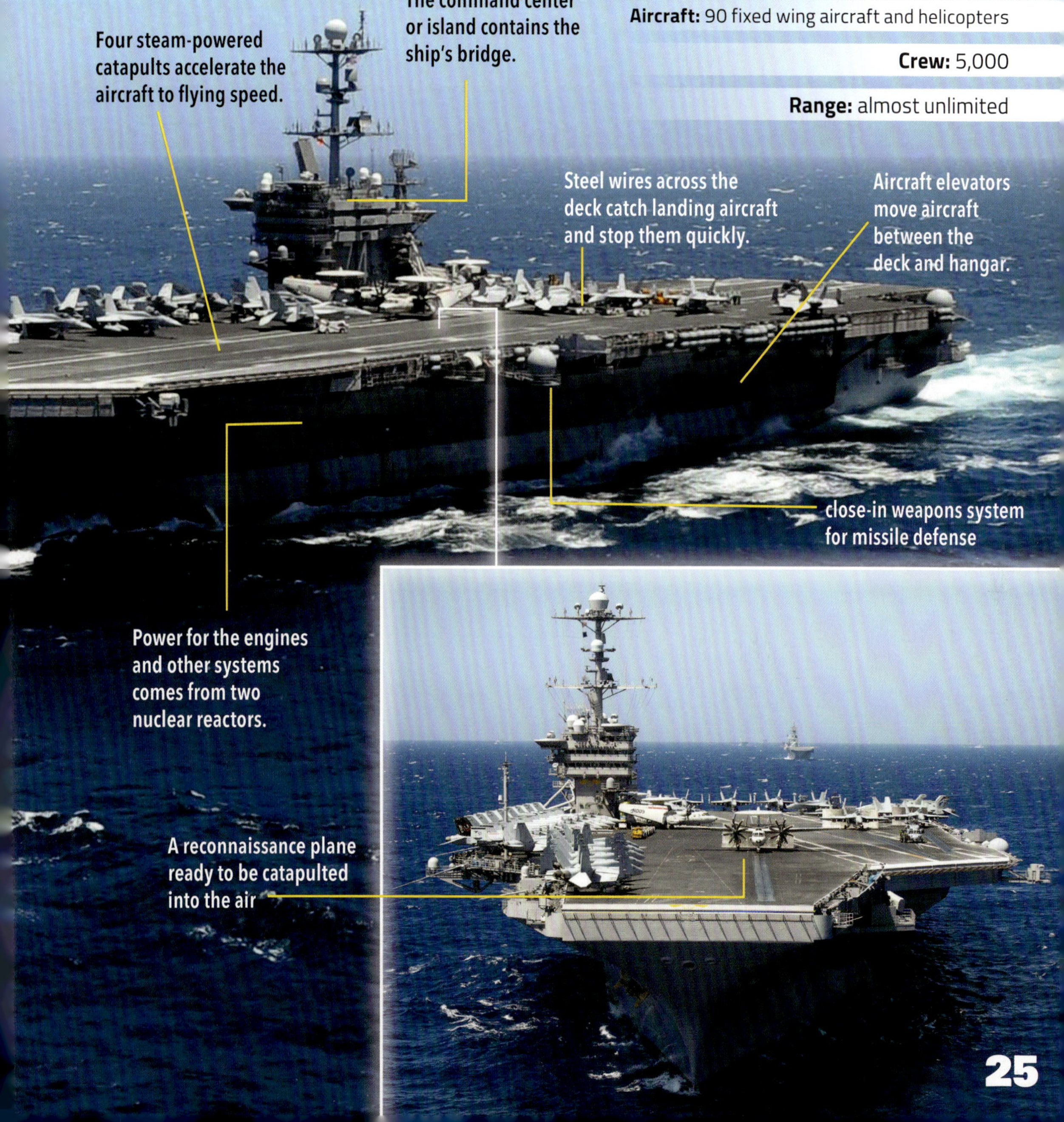

Four steam-powered catapults accelerate the aircraft to flying speed.

The command center or island contains the ship's bridge.

Steel wires across the deck catch landing aircraft and stop them quickly.

Aircraft elevators move aircraft between the deck and hangar.

close-in weapons system for missile defense

Power for the engines and other systems comes from two nuclear reactors.

A reconnaissance plane ready to be catapulted into the air.

25

INSIDE A WARSHIP

This is a modern warship of the British Navy. It's a Type 45 Destroyer—one of the most advanced warships in the world, full of high-tech equipment and weapons. It's a guided-missile destroyer, and its job is to protect aircraft carriers and other ships from aircraft and missile attack. Its radar can track two thousand targets at once, and it carries dozens of missiles to fire at approaching planes and missiles.

Operations Room

In the heart of the ship there is an operations room where the crew keeps an eye on enemy aircraft and ship movements. Information from the ship's radar, sonar, and other sensors is shown on screen. Missile launches and gunfire are controlled from here too.

The main gun fires twenty-five rounds a minute. It has ammunition storage in the depths of the ship. There are also other antiaircraft and machine guns for defending the ship.

Surface-to-air-missiles are stored in the missile silo.

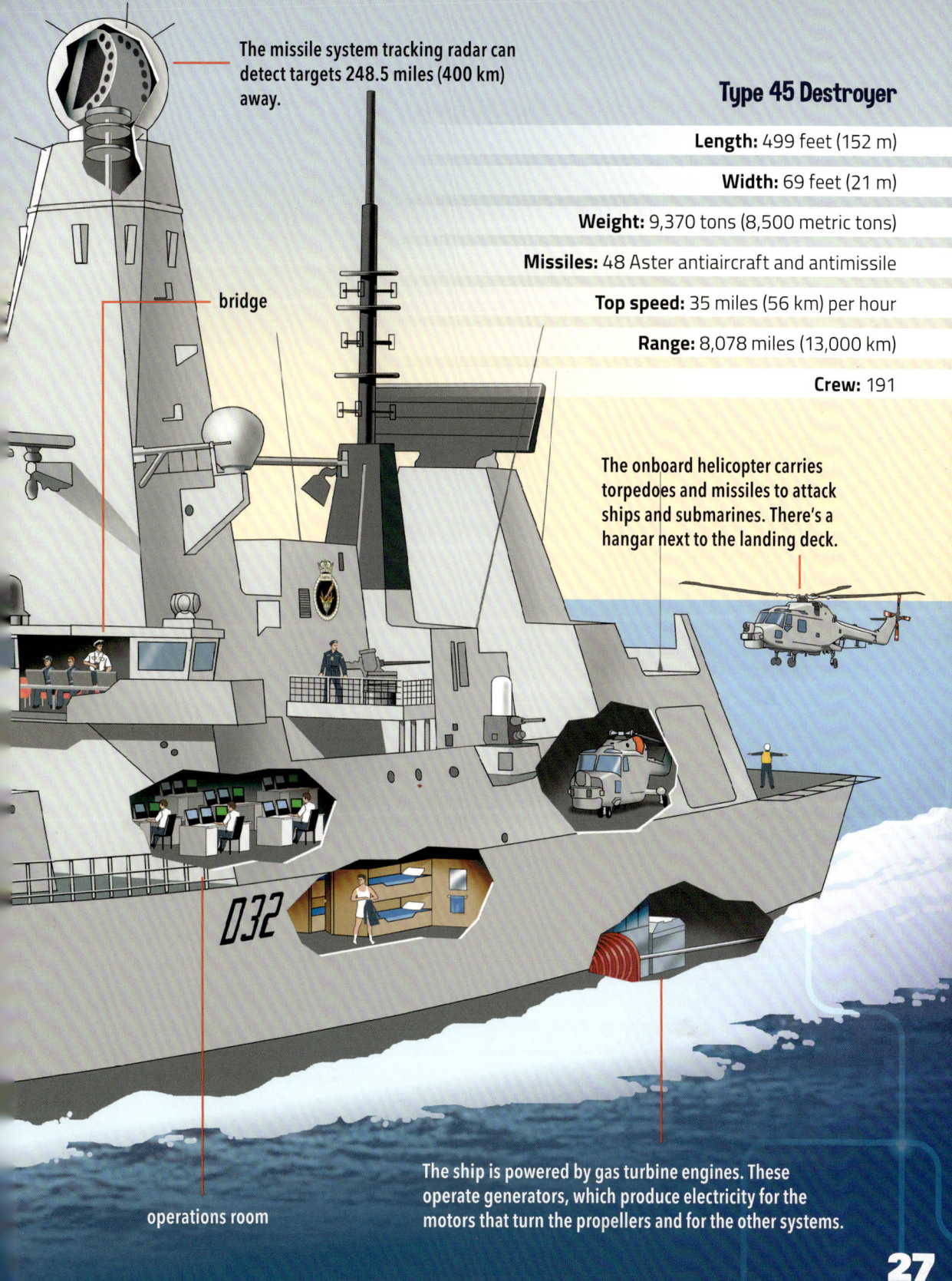

TIMELINE

10,000 BCE
By this time people were making journeys in simple boats.

1545
Henry VIII's warship the *Mary Rose* sinks during battle.

750 BCE
The Ancient Greeks develop the bireme, a galley with two sets of oars.

1588
The Spanish Armada, a great fleet of Spanish galleons, is defeated by English ships.

1805
British ships, led by HMS *Victory*, defeat a French and Spanish fleet at the Battle of Trafalgar.

1916
The British and German fleets meet at the Battle of Jutland, the only major naval battle of World War I.

1918
World War I ends.

1200
The stern rudder is developed in Europe, having previously been invented in China.

7th century CE
Greek fire, a weapon that sprays burning oil onto enemy ships, is invented.

480 BCE
The Greek navy defeats the larger Persian navy at the Battle of Salamis.

3,500 BCE
Evidence for the first sailing ships comes from this time.

1670
HMS *Prince*, a ship of Charles II of England, is launched.

16th century
Galleons, large fighting ships armed with cannons, are developed.

14th century
Cannons are used on ships for the first time.

1860s
In England, Robert Whitehead develops the torpedo.

1862
USS *Monitor* and CSS *Virginia* take shots at each other at the Battle of Hampton Roads, during the American Civil War.

1914
The battleship USS *Texas* enters service with the US Navy, as World War I begins in Europe.

1906
HMS *Dreadnought*, one of the first battleships, is launched.

1939-1945
Aircraft carriers and battleships play a major role in World War II.

2013
The US Navy's first stealth warship, the USS *Zumwalt*, is launched.

1972
USS *Nimitz*, the US Navy's first supercarrier, is launched.

FACT FILE

- At Trafalgar in 1805, the French and Spanish lost 22 of their 33 ships. The British lost none.

- There is evidence from Ancient Greece of truly giant triremes. One report describes a ship 426.5 feet (130 m) long, with hundreds of oars 59 feet (18 m) long, operated by 4,000 rowers.

- HMS *Victory*, a ship at the Battle of Trafalgar, had a top speed of 10 miles (16 km) per hour, which was very fast for a ship of its size.

- USS *Monitor* sank in a storm in 1862. Recently, parts of it have been raised from the seabed, including the rotating gun turret.

- The Spanish Armada was defeated by the weather as much as by English ships. Storms blew the Armada into the North Sea, and more storms destroyed up to half the ships.

- The USS *Zumwalt*, a US Navy stealth ship, has a low radar signature, so it looks like a small fishing boat on a radar screen.

- Around 250 ships, with a total of 100,000 crew onboard, took part in the Battle of Jutland in 1916, off the coast of Denmark. This image shows a German cruiser sinking (*right*).

GLOSSARY

Early naval mine

bow: the front of a ship

Confederate: one of the sides in the American Civil War. The other side was called the Union.

CSS: Confederate States Ship, a ship fighting for the Confederate forces during the American Civil War

frigate: the smallest but most common kind of modern warship

galleon: a large cargo and fighting ship of the fifteenth century, powered by wind

galley: an ancient type of warship, powered by many oars and a square sail

guided missile: a missile that is guided to its target by a laser or by detecting heat coming from a target

HMS: Her Majesty's Ship, a ship of the British Royal Navy

hull: the main body of a ship

ironclad: a warship with a wooden hull covered with iron plates for armor

keel: a strong structure along the bottom of a ship, like a spine

merchant ship: any non-naval ship

mine: an explosive device placed placed underwater that explodes when a ship hits it

missile: an object that is thrown or launched as a weapon, especially a rocket that explodes when it hits a target

Spanish galleon

rudder: a flap at the back of a ship used to make the ship turn left or right

steam turbine: a fan-like rotor that spins when steam flows through it

stern: the back of a ship

submersible: a small, often remote-controlled vessel that moves underwater

torpedo: a weapon fired from a ship or submarine that travels through the water to its target

USS: United States Ship, a ship of the US Navy

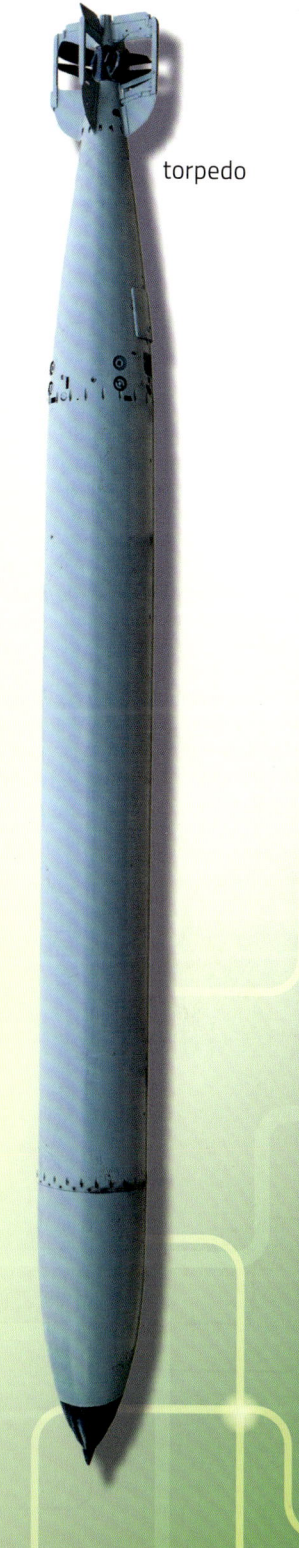

torpedo

USS *Cairo*, one of the first American ironclad warships

INDEX

aircraft carriers, 6, 20, 22, 24–26
American Civil War, 16–17
Ancient Greek warships, 8–11

Battle of Hampton Roads, 16
Battle of Salamis, 10–11
Battle of Trafalgar, 7, 14–15
battleships, 6–8, 18–20, 23
biremes, 9–10

cannons, 7, 12–13, 16–17, 23
carracks, 13
close in weapons system (CIWS), 23
CSS *Virginia*, 16–17

Egyptian warships, 8

galleons, 13–14
galleys, 8–11
Golden Hind, 13
Greek fire, 11

hangars, 21, 24
HMS *Dreadnought*, 18–19
HMS *Prince*, 15
HMS *Victory*, 7, 14

ironclads, 16–17

Nimitz-class supercarriers, 25

operations room, 26

shells, 16–18
ships of the line, 7, 14–15, 17
Spanish Armada, 12
stealth ships, 22
steam turbine engines, 18

torpedoes, 18–19
triremes, 8–10
Type 45 Destroyer, 26–27

uniremes, 9
USS *Monitor*, 16
USS *New Jersey*, 18
USS *Nimitz*, 7
USS *Texas*, 19
USS *Zumwalt*, 23

World War I, 18–20
World War II, 19–21

The Author

Chris Oxlade is an experienced author of educational books for children with more than two hundred titles to his name, including many on science and technology. He enjoys camping and adventurous outdoor sports, including rock climbing, hill running, kayaking, and sailing. He lives in England with his wife, children, and dogs.

Picture Credits (abbreviations: t = top; b = bottom; c = center; l = left; r = right)
© www.shutterstock.com: 4c, 8tl, 9tr, 12br, 18tl, 19c, 28tr, 28bc, 29br, 30tr, 30bl, 31bl, 31r

2, r = Cody Images. 3, c = Cody Images. 6–7, c = US Navy Photo / Alamy Stock Photo. 7, t = Niday Picture Library / Alamy Stock Photo. 8-9, c = Elena Elenaphotos21 / Alamy Stock Photo. 9, cl = Greek photonews / Alamy Stock Photo. 10, c = Bettmann / Getty Images. 12, c = National Geographic Creative / Alamy Stock Photo. 14, b = Maurice Savage / Alamy Stock Photo. 14-15, c = Glasshouse Images / Alamy Stock Photo. 16, tl = Ian Dagnall Computing / Alamy Stock Photo. 16-17, c = Archive Images / Alamy Stock Photo. 19, br = Stephen Barnes / Alamy Stock Photo. 20, c = Cody Images. 20, b = Cody Images. 21, t = Cody Images. 21, b = Cody Images. 22, c = WENN Ltd / Alamy Stock Photo. 23, t = Z2A Collection / Alamy Stock Photo. 23, b = Cody Images. 24, b = US Navy Photo / Alamy Stock Photo. 24-25, c = Stocktrek Images, Inc. /Alamy Stock Photo. 26, cl = IAP / Alamy Stock Photo. 29, c = Niday Picture Library / Alamy Stock Photo.

623.825 O FLT
Oxlade, Chris,
Inside battleships :an Iowa-class
 World War II battleship fires her g

04/18